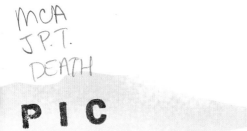

FRENCH TOAST
SUNDAYS

By Gloria Spielman

Illustrated by Inbal Gigi Bousidan

APPLES & HONEY PRESS

French toast and Sundays
had always gone together,
like peanut butter and jelly or
apples and honey – and you
couldn't have French Toast
Sundays without Grandma.

On French Toast Sundays Grandma
would ask Mina to tie her apron.

"Not too tight. Not too loose.
Just right."

And they would get down to the business of beating those eggs as hard as they could.

A pinch of this. Not quite right. A shake of that. Mmm, just right.

Beat, dip. Fry.

"Not too crispy. Not too soft. Mmm, just right."

Then they would take their plates into the yard
and Mina would shimmy up the old tree, climb
onto her favorite branch and settle into the little
nook in its gnarled trunk.

"Come on up,
Grandma,"
Mina would say.

"No, thank you, dear.
I'm staying right here."

And that's how Sunday
mornings had been for as
long as Mina remembered.

But this Sunday, Aunt Jan
was in the kitchen.

Mom and Uncle Al were wearing ripped shirts, and people were telling them that they were so sorry. There were boiled eggs instead of French toast, and on the windowsill burned a candle.

"I hate boiled eggs," yelled Mina
and ran outside to the old tree.

Up, up, up she climbed
to her favorite branch.

On Monday, Mrs. Davis arrived with a pot of hot vegetable soup and a mushroom pie. More people came to sit with Mom and Uncle Al. In and out they came, all day long. They talked. They cried. Sometimes they laughed. Mina watched.

She didn't talk. She didn't laugh. Sometimes she cried.

Too busy. Too noisy. Just too much.

"Come on down, Mina," said Aunt Jan.

"Staying right here," said Mina.

And in the evening the house filled with people who came to say prayers for Grandma.

On Tuesday, Mr. Ellman brought
a dish of bubbling hot lasagna.

"We got ourselves into some right old pickles in
grade school. One summer I dared her to climb the
biggest oak in the park. She didn't tell me she was
scared of heights. She got into a fine flap.

The park ranger had
to carry her down.
She swore she'd never
climb another tree as
long as she lived."

"How about that?"
Mom smiled and took
a sip of tea.

Mina inched a little
further down the tree.

On Wednesday, Mr. Rosen brought a pan of crispy fried chicken. Aunt Jan went in and out of the kitchen with cups of tea. The house was busy all day long.

On Thursday, Mrs. Ellman brought her famous apple strudel.

"Thought you might like this," said Mr. Green. "That there's your mother."

"Mom never rode a motorcycle!" said Uncle Al.

"She sure did," said Mr. Green. "All the way to Brighton Beach!"

"Who knew?" said Uncle Al, and took a bite of strudel.

Mina swung onto the branch below, dropped onto the porch, and squished her nose right up against the windowpane.

On Friday, Mrs. Gutman brought a tureen of soup, baked fish and a bowl of steaming carrots.

"I'll say one thing," said Uncle Al.
"She was a terrible cook!"

"She certainly was," said Mom.
"But she made a mean French toast."

"Sure did." Uncle Al smiled. "And
she never told us how she made it.
A secret, she said."

"Wish we knew," said Mom.

Mina went into the kitchen. She asked Aunt Jan to tie her apron.

"Not too tight.
Not too loose.
Just right."

And she got down to the business of
beating those eggs as hard as she could.

Beat, dip. Fry.

Not too crispy, not too soft. Mmm, just right.

"Thought you might like this," said Mina
to Mom and Uncle Al.

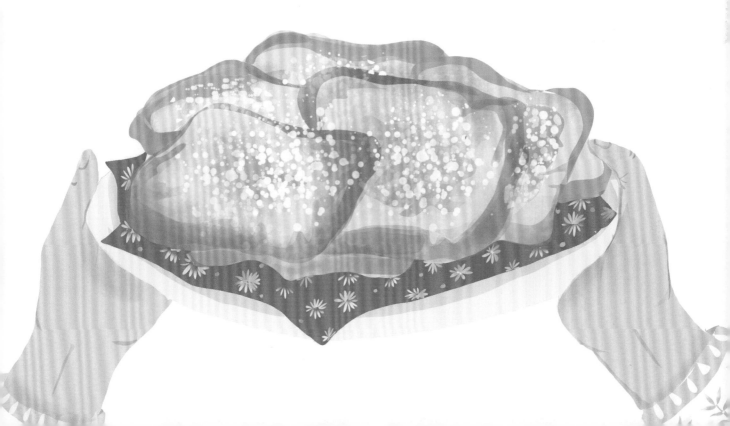

"Delicious," said Uncle Al. "Just like she used to make."

"Superb," said Mom. "Grandma told you her secret?"

"She sure did," said Mina.
"Who knew?" said Uncle Al.

They smiled.
Then they laughed.
Right out loud.

NOTE TO FAMILIES

Sometimes when someone we love dies, we are so sad we can't put it into words. We just feel lost without them. In Jewish tradition, friends and family come to visit the mourners, bringing comfort, prayer, and food for seven days. We light a candle, eat boiled eggs, and tear the clothes we are wearing. During this time, which is called *shiva*, Mina is able to feel her grief and draw closer to the people who loved her Grandma, by remembering together that those we loved are always around us.

In memory of my dear mother-in-law, Dorothy Frankel Wexler –GS

For my parents, my husband and my boys—and Amanda, who gave me the golden key –IGB

Apples & Honey Press
Springfield, NJ 07081
www.applesandhoneypress.com

Text copyright © 2018 by Gloria Spielman
Illustrations copyright © 2018 by Inbal Gigi Bousidan

ISBN 978-1-68115-529-6

Library of Congress Cataloging-in-Publication Data
Names: Spielman, Gloria, author. | Gigi Bousidan, Inbal, illustrator.
Title: French toast Sundays / by Gloria Spielman ; illustrated by Inbal Gigi Bousidan.
Description: Springfield, New Jersey : Apples & Honey Press, 2018. | Summary:
After the loss of her beloved grandmother, Mina finds solace in stories told by family and friends,
but her grief is turned into joy when she surprises everyone with Grandma's famous French toast.
Identifiers: LCCN 2016051153 | ISBN 9781681155296
Subjects: | CYAC: Grandmothers--Fiction. | Death--Fiction. | Grief--Fiction. | Jews--United States--Fiction.
Classification: LCC PZ7.1.S71454 Fr 2018 | DDC [E]--dc23 LC record available at https://lccn.loc.gov/2016051153

Design by Virtual Paintbrush | Editor: Amanda Cohen

Printed in China
1 3 5 7 9 8 6 4 2